Have You Fed the Cat?

To my Dad, Stan Kelly-Bootle, and my Mum, Peggy Bootle,
with love and best wishes

First published in the United States of America in 2004 by Star Bright Books, New York. Published in the United Kingdom by Happy Cat Books.

The name Star Bright Books and the Star Bright Books logo are registered trademarks of Star Bright Books, Inc. Please visit www.starbrightbooks.com.

Hardcover ISBN 1-932065-90-3   Printed in China
Paperback ISBN 1-932065-91-1   0 9 8 7 6 5 4 3 2 1

Library of Congress Cataloging-in-Publication Data

Coxon, Michèle.
  Have you fed the cat? / Michele Coxon.
     p. cm.
  Summary: When Sam the cat becomes too big to fit through the cat flap, the Robinson family realizes that even though they have been feeding him, they have neglected him in other ways.
   ISBN 1-932065-90-3 (hardcover) -- ISBN 1-932065-91-1 (pbk.)
  [1. Cats--Fiction. 2. Pets--Fiction. 3. Responsibility--Fiction.] I. Title.
PZ7.C83945Ha 2004
[E]--dc22   2004008687.

Have You Fed the Cat?

Michèle Coxon

STAR BRIGHT BOOKS

NEW YORK

When Sam came to live with the Robinsons, he was a tiny, tabby kitten. The children, Rose and Charlie, loved him and stroked his soft fur. They told him how beautiful he was and Sam purred happily.

Together they played pouncing and jumping games. Whenever Charlie pulled yarn through the grass, Sam leaped on it. He flew into the air to catch the balls that Rose threw.

"You are so clever," said Rose.
"And so beautiful," added Charlie.
"I know," purred Sam.

Sam grew into a beautiful long-haired cat. The children also grew and became too busy for games and cat-stroking.

"I'm lonely," thought Sam, as he cleaned his bottom. "The only time they pay attention to me is when I meow for food."

Sam was good at asking for food. He would stand in the middle of the kitchen until somebody almost tripped over him. When Charlie came back, tired and muddy from soccer practice, Sam wailed, "I'm hungry! Feed me!" To get some peace, Charlie filled his dish with food.

"Give me some food!" Sam meowed at Rose as he lay across the keyboard of her computer. Rose wanted to play her new game, so she fed him.

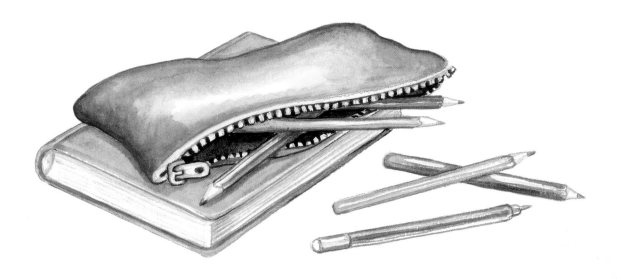

"I'm starving! Feed me!" begged Sam as he stood in front of the television. Mom fed him so she could watch her favorite program.

"No one has fed me!" Sam meowed sadly as he tore a hole in Dad's newspaper. Dad put down his paper and got the cat food out.

"The Robinsons never feed me!" wailed
Sam as he got under Mrs. Jones's feet.
"I'm here to clean the house, not feed the
cat," muttered Mrs. Jones, but she fed him
so that she could tidy up in peace.

Sam grew fatter and fatter and fatter –
but no one noticed because of his long fur.
Then, one day, he got stuck in his cat-flap!
He cried so loudly that everyone came running.

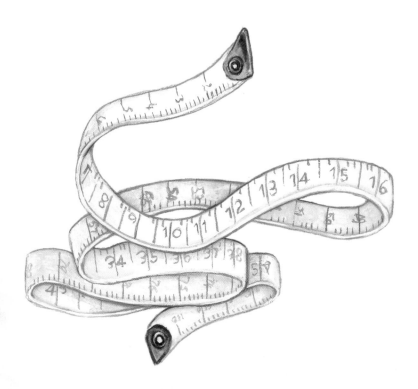

"How on earth did you get so fat?" asked Mom as she pulled him out from the back.

"I don't feed him much," said Charlie.

"I only give him one plateful," added Rose.

"Just half a tin," agreed Dad.

"Same here," said Mrs. Jones.

"Oh no!" cried Mom. "We've *all* been feeding him!"

"It's back to two meals a day for you, Sam," she said. "I will feed you and the children can get you into shape."

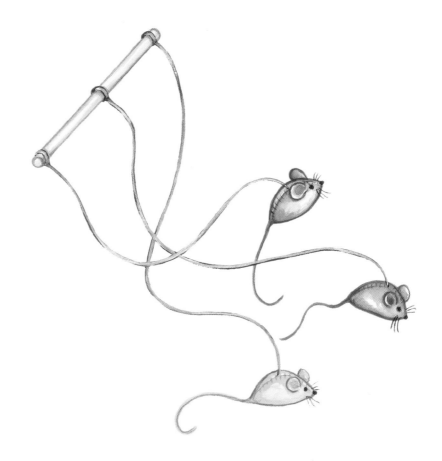

Over the next few months Sam didn't have much time to think about food. Getting in shape meant fun and games with his family. As he lost weight, he could pounce more quickly and leap much higher. The children laughed and clapped and told him how beautiful and clever he was.

At bathtime, the children blew bubbles for Sam to catch. "We almost forgot how much fun you can be!" laughed Charlie.

And from then on Sam had lots to do and two good meals a day. . .

Apart from the occasional snack!